THE USBORNE YOUNG CARTOONIST

Part One
HOW TO DRAW CARTOONS AND CARICATURES
Judy Tatchell

Designed by Graham Round

Illustrated by Graham Round, Terry Bave, Robert Walster and Chris Lyon

Additional designs by Brian Robertson and Camilla Luff

Contents

2 About part one
3 First faces
4 Cartoon people
6 Making faces
8 Drawing caricatures
10 Drawing from different sides
12 Moving pictures
14 More movement
16 Drawing stereotypes
18 Cartoons growing up
20 Scenery and perspective
22 Cartoon jokes
24 Strip cartoons
26 Comic strips
28 Special effects
30 Cartoon story books
32 Drawing animals
34 How cartoon films are made
38 Mix and match
40 Cartoons and real people

Consultants: Terry and Shiela Bave

About part one

Caricature

The first part of this book is all about how to draw cartoons. It is full of simple methods you can use and lots of pictures to copy and give you ideas.

The next few pages tell you how to draw cartoon people using simple shapes and lines. You can find out how to draw movement and expressions, too.

A caricature is a funny picture of a real person. You exaggerate things, such as the shape of their nose or hair. You can find out how to do this on pages 8-9.

A cartoon story book.

YAP!

A strip cartoon is a series of pictures which tell a joke or funny short story. You can find out how to build up your own strip cartoons on pages 24-25.

Looking at a cartoon story book is a bit like watching a film and reading a book at the same time. You can see how the Tintin stories were created on pages 30-31.

On pages 34-37, you can find out how cartoon films are made. This is called animation, which means "the giving of life". Cartoons are brought to life in a film.

First faces

This page shows you an easy way to draw cartoon faces. All you need is a pencil and a sheet of paper. If you want to colour the faces in, you can use crayons or felt tips.

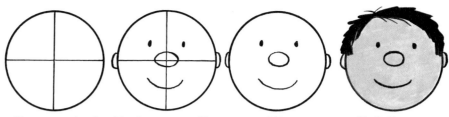

Draw a circle. Do two pencil lines crossing it. Put the nose where the lines cross. The ears are level with the nose. The eyes go slightly above the nose. Rub out the lines crossing the face. Add any sort of hair you like.

Faces to copy

Here are some more faces for you to copy. You can see how in a cartoon some things are exaggerated, such as the size of the nose or the expression.

Looking around

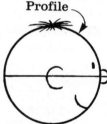

Draw these lines in pencil so you can rub them out later.

Nose goes where lines cross.

Ear moves round.

As the face turns more, this line moves further round.

Profile

The first picture shows a face from the front, with lines crossing it.

As the face looks to the side, the line going across the face stays where it is. The line going down curves to one side. The curve of the line makes the head look ball-shaped.

This is a side view, or profile. Draw a line across the middle of the head to show you where the nose and ears go.

Line curves up in the middle.

The more line curves, the higher person looks.

Line curves down in the middle.

To draw a face looking up, do a line across the face as shown. The nose goes in the centre and the ears at each end of the line.

For a face looking down, the line curves down in the middle. Can you see how the face looking up and to one side is drawn?

3

Cartoon people

Now you can try adding some bodies to your cartoon faces. There are two different methods described on these pages. The first uses stick figures. The second uses rounded shapes. Try them both and see which you find easier.

Stick figures

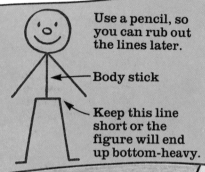

Use a pencil, so you can rub out the lines later.

Body stick

Keep this line short or the figure will end up bottom-heavy.

Rub out a bit of the head line here, where the hair falls forward.

Draw this stick figure. The body stick is slightly longer than the head. The legs are slightly longer than the body. The arms are a little shorter than the legs.

Here are the outlines of some clothes for the figure. You can copy a sweatshirt with jeans or with a skirt. You could also try some dungarees or a dress.

To dress your stick figure, draw the clothes round it, starting at the neck and working down.

You can add long, short, curly or straight hair.

Drawing hands and feet

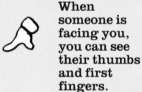

When someone is facing you, you can see their thumbs and first fingers.

People's feet usually turn out a bit.

Cartoon hands and shoes, like cartoon heads, are larger than on a real person. Practise drawing these shapes before you add them to the figures.

Colouring in

Use a fine felt tip pen for the outline.

A cartoon person's head is larger than on a real person.

Give her socks if you like.

Shiny white patch on shoes.

When you have finished the outline of the figure, go over it with a felt tip pen. When it is dry you can rub out the stick figure and colour the cartoon in.

The girl needs some lines for legs before you can put on her shoes. When you colour the shoes, leave a small, white patch on the toes to make them shiny.

Figures using rounded shapes

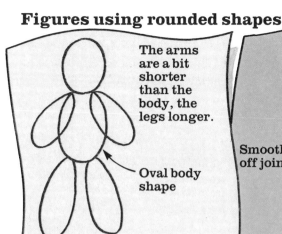

The arms are a bit shorter than the body, the legs longer.

Oval body shape

Smoothed-off join.

These stripes are slightly curved to show the rounded shape of the body.

With a pencil, draw a head shape. Add an oval for the body shape and sausages for the arms and legs. The body is about one and a half times as long as the head.

Add the outlines of the clothes, smoothing off any joins, such as between the arms or legs and the body. Go over the outline in ink and rub out pencil lines.

Add hands and feet and colour the figure in.

You can find out how to make your cartoon figure look as if it is moving on pages 12-15.

More cartoon people to draw

Try varying your rounded shapes or stick figures to draw different-shaped cartoon people.

Tiny person. Head larger in proportion to body.

Tall person. Egg-shaped head and longer body.

Fat person. Head squashed and legs shorter.

Short person. Head, body and legs the same length.

Some things to try

When you have practised drawing several figures using the methods shown above, you could try drawing a figure outline straight off. If you find it difficult, you can go back to drawing a stick or rounded shape figure first.

Try drawing these different people:
- A fat lady in a fur coat and hat.
- A man with hairy legs in shorts.
- A boy and a girl wearing party clothes.

5

Making faces

You can make cartoon characters come to life by giving them different expressions. These two pages show you how to do this, by adding or changing a few lines. First, try the faces in pencil. Then you can colour them in.

Happy faces

Girls and women tend to have slightly smaller noses than boys and men.

These lines make the ears look more real. →

Happiness is shown by a smiling mouth. Drawing the eyes as shown above gives a cheerful expression.

You can make the person burst out laughing by opening the mouth more and showing the teeth.

This is a bigger laugh. The head is thrown back. You can find out how to position the features on page 3.

Sad and angry faces

Sadness and anger are also mainly shown in the eyes and mouth.

Lines show shaking with fury.

Sad: the mouth and eyebrows droop.

Angry: use straight lines for the mouth and eyebrows.

Furious: the person frowns and goes red in the face.

Hopping mad: the mouth is wide open in a loud yell.

More expressions

Here are lots more expressions for you to copy and practise.

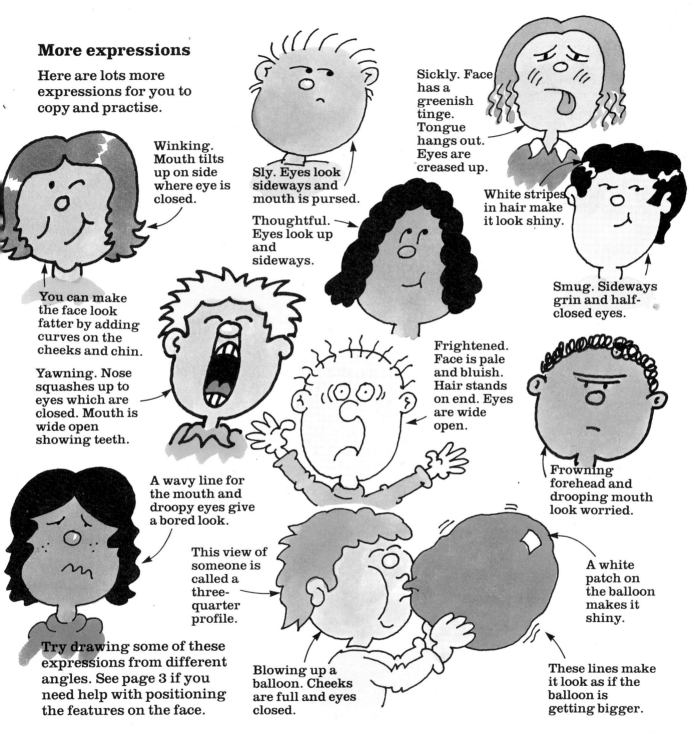

Winking. Mouth tilts up on side where eye is closed.

Sly. Eyes look sideways and mouth is pursed.

Sickly. Face has a greenish tinge. Tongue hangs out. Eyes are creased up.

White stripes in hair make it look shiny.

Thoughtful. Eyes look up and sideways.

Smug. Sideways grin and half-closed eyes.

You can make the face look fatter by adding curves on the cheeks and chin.

Yawning. Nose squashes up to eyes which are closed. Mouth is wide open showing teeth.

Frightened. Face is pale and bluish. Hair stands on end. Eyes are wide open.

Frowning forehead and drooping mouth look worried.

A wavy line for the mouth and droopy eyes give a bored look.

This view of someone is called a three-quarter profile.

A white patch on the balloon makes it shiny.

Try drawing some of these expressions from different angles. See page 3 if you need help with positioning the features on the face.

Blowing up a balloon. Cheeks are full and eyes closed.

These lines make it look as if the balloon is getting bigger.

Drawing caricatures

A caricature is a picture of someone which exaggerates their most striking or unusual features. Although a caricature looks funny, you can recognize the person easily.

It helps to look at the person, or at a photograph of them, while you are drawing.

Caricatured features

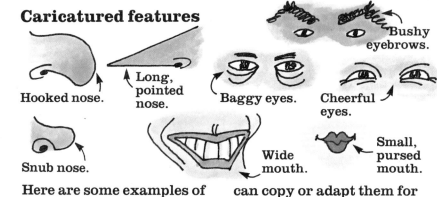

Hooked nose.

Long, pointed nose.

Snub nose.

Bushy eyebrows.

Baggy eyes.

Cheerful eyes.

Wide mouth.

Small, pursed mouth.

Here are some examples of caricatured features. You can copy or adapt them for your own caricatures.

Tricks of the trade

Imagine the features you would pick out if you were describing the person to someone else. These are the features to exaggerate.

Here are some caricatures drawn from photographs. Try copying them.

Draw lines to help position eyes, nose and ears.

Put ears and nose below line going across face.

Add spectacles.

Exaggerate chin, cheeks and bushy eyebrows.

Draw lines to help position eyes, nose and mouth.

Draw in nose, eyes and mouth. Do round cheeks.

Main features are lots of fluffy hair and a long fringe.

Draw a face shape and lines. Add ear and earring.

Do small, turned-up nose, glasses, and mouth.

Main features are cheeks, spiky hair and glasses.

 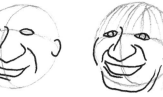  

Head is long and wedge-shaped rather than round.

Draw in a long nose, a smile, an ear and eyes.

Main features are cheeks, long chin and fluffy hair.

Round head. Lines show where eyes and nose go.

Draw a big nose, a grin, eyes and chubby cheeks.

Make chin a bit longer. Do a long fringe over eyes.

Caricature yourself

You can draw a funny caricature of yourself by looking at yourself in a shiny spoon. The curve of the spoon distorts your features.

If you look in the back of the spoon, your nose looks very big.

Turn the spoon sideways to get a different effect.

9

Drawing from different sides

Here you can find out how to draw people from the side and from the back as well as from the front.

You can also see how to make your pictures look interesting by drawing, say, a bird's eye view. There are some instructions for how to do this on the opposite page.

Turning round

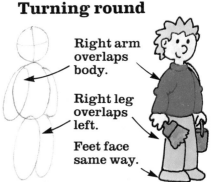

Right arm overlaps body.

Right leg overlaps left.

Feet face same way.

As a person begins to turn round, their body gets narrower. (See page 3 for how to draw the face.)

Side view

Arm towards back of body.

Back of hand.

Left leg just visible behind right.

Shape of nose

From the side, the body is at its narrowest. You can see the shape of the nose and the back of one hand.

Back view

You can see the backs of the heels.

From the back, the body parts are the same sizes and shapes as from the front.

More positions to draw

Here are lots of cartoon people, in all sorts of positions. Copy them and they will help you draw people in other positions, too.

Sitting on the ground.

Piggy-back

On a bicycle.

Sitting on a chair.

Drawing a bird's eye view

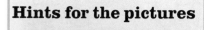

A bird's eye view can make an ordinary picture look quite dramatic. Try drawing this queue.

The parts of the body nearer to you are bigger than those further away. Also, the bodies are shorter than if you were drawing them from straight on. This is called foreshortening.

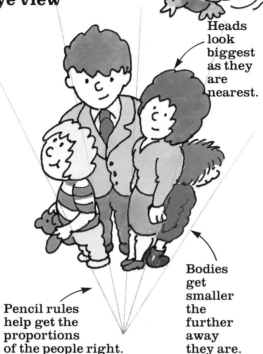

Heads look biggest as they are nearest.

Bodies get smaller the further away they are.

Draw a set of pencil rules fanning out from a point. Fit the people roughly in between them.

Pencil rules help get the proportions of the people right.

A worm's eye view

Bodies get smaller the further away they are and they are foreshortened.

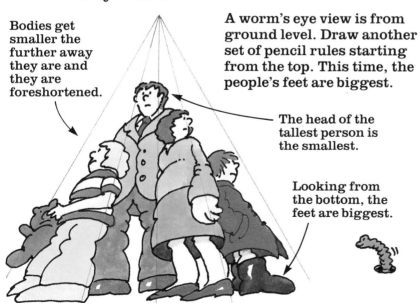

A worm's eye view is from ground level. Draw another set of pencil rules starting from the top. This time, the people's feet are biggest.

The head of the tallest person is the smallest.

Looking from the bottom, the feet are biggest.

11

Moving pictures

Here, you can find out how to draw cartoon people walking, running, jumping and so on. Start with a stick or shape figure if it helps.

Walking and running

The right arm is in front when the left leg is forward.

Stick figure to help you get the body right.

When someone is walking briskly, they lean forwards slightly. There is always one foot on the ground.

Draw the figure just above ground level to show he is on the move.

Starting to run, the body leans forwards even more. The elbows bend and move backwards and forwards.

Add a few curved lines to show fast movement.

Blobs of sweat flying off head.

The faster someone is going, the more the body leans forwards and the further the arms stretch.

Jumping

The more this leg bends, the higher the jump will be.

Both feet come forward to hit the ground.

Running towards the jump . . .

Taking off . . .

In mid-flight . . .

Landing from the jump.

Falling over

These pictures show a stick person running along and tripping over. Copy them and then fill in the body shapes around the stick figures.

Action pictures

Here are lots of action pictures to try. There are stick figures next to each picture, to help you get the body right. Look at page 4 if you need reminding how long each part of the body should be.

Hitting

These curved lines show the swing of the racket.

Throwing

These lines show the path of the ball.

Diving

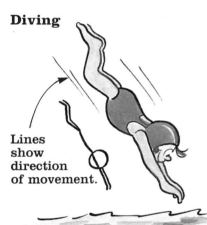

Lines show direction of movement.

Swimming

Add lots of splashes and movement lines.

Rollerskating

Arm stretched out in front.

Rollerskating is similar to running but there is always a foot on the ground.

Skateboarding

Body leaning back and legs bent.

You can get a good sense of turning a corner fast by bending the body and legs.

Kicking

When kicking a ball, the body twists towards the foot that is kicking.

13

More movement

Here are some even more dramatic ways to show movement. You exaggerate certain things to give an impression of lots of speed or effort. You can write words on a picture to give extra impact.

Beads of perspiration.

Fists clenched.

Legs spinning.

Clouds of dust.

You can even add movement lines round the letters.

ZOOM!

Make the letters big and bold. You could do them in colour.

This is someone running to catch a bus. You can add a word like ZOOM or WHIZZ, with an exclamation mark.

ZIP !

Wheel spin.

The hair and scarf of the skater on the left are streaming out behind her. This gives a sense of speed.

These figures look like they are running away. The dust clouds get smaller as they get further away.* The

figures are in the distance, so they are small. A curved line for the ground gives a feeling of space.

These silhouettes have long shadows to make it look like evening.

14   *This is called perspective. There is more about it on pages 20-21 and 59.*

Freeze-frame pictures

You can draw pictures that look frozen in the middle of exciting action, as if you were freezing a video during a film. You do this by adding details of moving things, such as those in the pictures here.

Wide mouth and eyes and spinning head make him look dazed.

Ski pole flying through the air makes it look like the accident has just happened.

Snow swooshing up as skier comes to a sudden halt.

Boy's wallet falling from his pocket.

You could copy this picture, but try drawing different costumes, hairstyles and expressions.

Girl's drink spilling.

An action scene to try

These lines make it look like the person is somersaulting.

Try drawing someone trampolining. They might get into all sorts of positions in the air.

Some freeze-frame ideas

Scenes where there is a lot of action are good for freeze-frame pictures.

You could try an ice-rink, a windy day, or a party by a swimming pool.

15

Drawing stereotypes

As well as drawing caricatures of real people (see pages 8-9), you can draw caricatures of different types of people, such as a burglar or a chef. These are called stereotypes. They are not pictures of real people but you can recognize from the pictures what sort of people they are or what they do for a living.

You normally recognize a stereotype from the shape of the body and the clothes. Here are some to try.

Getting started

If you like, draw stick figures or rounded shapes to help you get started on the figure. There is more about this on pages 4-5. Then you can work on the outline and clothes.

Can you see which pictures on these two pages the shapes above belong to?

Chef

Chef's hat

Light blue shading on the clothes gives the impression of whiteness.

A stereotyped chef is jolly and round, with a big red face and a moustache.

Burglar

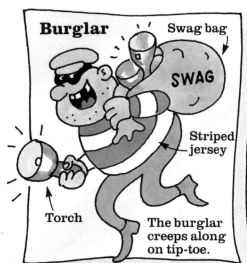

Swag bag

SWAG

Striped jersey

Torch

The burglar creeps along on tip-toe.

No real burglar would wear this kind of outfit, but this is how they are often drawn in cartoons.

Boxer

Head protected by hands.

Opponent knocked out.

The boxer is muscular and heavy, with a squashy nose and swollen ear. He wears big gloves and laced boots.

Ballerina

These lines show she is pirouetting.

Slender limbs and hands.

The ballerina is very slim and light on her feet. She stands on her toes.

Spy

The spy's hat is pulled down and the collar of his coat is turned up. One furtive eye looks out from under the brim of his hat.

Pop star

A pop star wears trendy clothes and jewellery. Draw her mouth open and coloured lights behind her.

Soccer player

A soccer player looks fit and energetic. You can draw him wearing your favourite team's strip.

Jockey

Jodphurs

Riding crop

A jockey is small, wiry and bow-legged. He wears a peaked hat with the brim turned up and racing colours on his clothes.

Gangster

Dark glasses

A gangster wears smart clothes, smokes a cigar and carries a violin case to conceal his gun.

More stereotypes

Clown

Cowboy

Fairytale princess

Witch

Butler

Here are some ideas for some more stereotypes. Can you think of others?

17

Cartoons growing up

As people grow older, their bodies change shape. So does the way they stand, sit and move.

These pages show some of the tricks involved in drawing people of different ages.

Babies

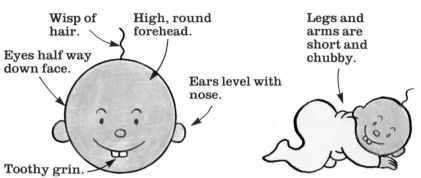

Wisp of hair.

High, round forehead.

Eyes half way down face.

Ears level with nose.

Toothy grin.

Legs and arms are short and chubby.

You can exaggerate the size of the mouth.

Babies sit with their legs straight out.

The face shape is a circle. The features are all in the lower half of the face.

A baby's shape is rounded with a large head, a bulge for a nappy and short limbs.

A baby's head is about one third of the whole length of the body.

Children

Eyebrows placed well above the eyes make the eyes look open and lively.

A lopsided grin looks cheeky.

Children's bodies are still quite rounded.

Children's heads are still quite large in proportion to the rest of the body.

Ears and nose half way down head.

Eyes slightly above line of ears.

There is slightly more space between the chin and mouth on a child than on a baby.

Girls' and boys' faces are similar shapes but they can have different hairstyles.

As a child grows, the limbs get longer in proportion to the rest of the body.

Men and women

Tufts of hair show man is going slightly bald.

Eyes above line of ears and nose.

Round eyebrows give a softer shape.

Neater hairstyle than girl.

A woman's body is more rounded than a man's.

The head is just under a quarter of the length of the body.

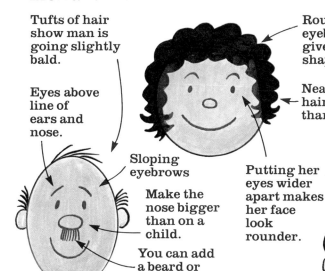

Sloping eyebrows

Make the nose bigger than on a child.

Putting her eyes wider apart makes her face look rounder.

You can add a beard or moustache.

Make the man's face more of an oval shape than a circle, and sharper at the chin.

A woman's face is usually rounder than a man's. Draw it as a circle.

An adult's legs are just under half the length of the whole body.

Old people

Hair grows further back on head.

An old man's body is quite angular.

You can make people look older by giving them spectacles or walking sticks.

Small eyes and sloping eyebrows.

Bald head.

Ears low down on the side of the head.

An old woman's body is more rounded.

Toothy grin

An old person's face is round, like a baby's. It has other similar features.

Old people tend to be bent over. Their heads are placed further forwards.

Old people are usually smaller and more fragile than younger adults.

Scenery and perspective

Scenery and backgrounds can add a lot of information about what is happening in your pictures. You need to keep the scenery quite simple, though, so that characters stand out against it.

Here, you can see how to get a sense of distance, or depth, into pictures. This is called drawing in perspective.*

Tricks of perspective

The further away something is, the smaller it looks. The woman in this picture is drawn smaller than the burglar to make her look further away.

Draw the woman further up the picture than the burglar. Otherwise it will look like the picture above. She just looks like a tiny person.

Parallel lines appear to get closer the further away they are. They seem to meet on the horizon. This point is called the vanishing point.

A high vanishing point makes it seem as if you are looking down on the picture. What happens if you draw a low vanishing point?

A picture in perspective

Here is a picture in perspective. The woman is drawn smaller and further up than the burglar to make her look further away.

Fence posts get closer together.

Pavement and fence get narrower.

If the vanishing point falls outside your picture area, try sketching it in pencil as above. This helps to get all the lines properly in perspective. You can rub the lines out later.

Adding depth

Lines going across a picture can also add depth. Here, the lines of hills make it look as if the scenery goes back for miles.

See how the road gets narrower in perspective as it gets further away, and the birds get smaller.

Scenery gets paler and less distinct the further away it is.

The man is large because he is nearest to you.

◄ In this picture, the curved lines of the circus arena show the depth of the picture.

Colour and shape are less distinct the further away they are, so only the front row of people are drawn in. Coloured blobs suggest the rest of the crowd.

Drawing objects

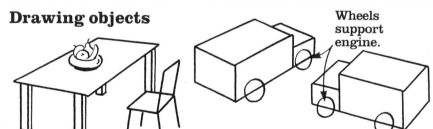

Wheels support engine.

Rub out these lines.

Square or oblong objects, such as tables and chairs, are quite easy to draw in perspective. The opposite sides are almost parallel.

You can draw a more complicated object, such as a car, by first constructing it out of a number of box shapes.

Then round off the corners and add the details. You may need to practise this a bit. Looking at an object while you draw it can help.

Cartoon jokes

Cartoon jokes are often printed in black and white in newspapers and magazines. They may be in the form of a strip (see pages 24-25) or a single picture, called a single cartoon. The one on the right is a single cartoon.

Here you can find out what kind of jokes make good cartoons, what materials cartoonists use and some tips on drawing single cartoons yourself.

What makes a good single cartoon?

Visual, that is, a lot of the humour and information about what is happening is in the picture.
A short caption.
A joke that is quick and easy to get.

The type of joke that makes a good single cartoon usually has the qualities shown above.

Ideas for jokes

It can be difficult to think up ideas for jokes on the spot. It helps to think first of a theme or situation. This may then suggest something funny to you.

Here are some common cartoon themes and some jokes based on them.

A desert island

This is probably the most common theme for single cartoon jokes.

A hospital

GET YOUR ACCIDENT INSURANCE HERE

This joke has two common cartoon themes – hospitals and manhole covers.

Vampires

This is funny because it shows a monstrous creature doing something ordinary.

Drawing materials*

The materials shown below are enough to get you started. You may already have them. If you like, though, you can buy the more specialized materials shown on the rest of this page.

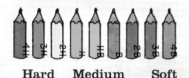

Hard   Medium   Soft

Pencils are marked to show how hard or soft they are. Experiment to find a type you like. Pencils range from 9B (very soft) to 9H (very hard).

You can draw on good quality typing paper which is quite cheap.

Fibre tip pens do not smudge or blot. In time, though, the ink fades in daylight. If you find it easier, sketch a drawing in pencil first and then ink over it. You can cover mistakes with typewriter correction fluid.

How professional cartoonists work

Single cartoons are drawn in black and white for printing in newspapers and magazines. Here are some of the materials that cartoonists use. You could try some of them yourself.

Pencils. The artist might use a medium pencil for outlines and a softer one for shading.

Fine paintbrushes

Art board. This can have different surfaces from very smooth and shiny to quite rough and soft.

Fibre tip pens

Drawing pens. These come with different thicknesses of nib. They draw a very even line.

Dip pens and Indian ink. You can get different shapes and thicknesses of nib.

Cartridge paper takes pens, pencils or paint equally well.

Fountain pens

Cartoons are mostly printed quite small. They are usually drawn larger than final size and reduced photographically before printing.

The cartoonist is told what size the cartoon will be printed.

By drawing a diagonal line across a box that size, the artist can scale the size up so that it is larger but still the same shape.

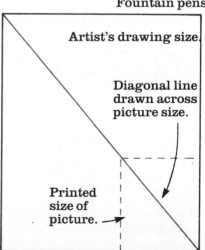

Artist's drawing size.

Diagonal line drawn across picture size.

Printed size of picture.

There is a chart showing lots of drawing and painting materials on pages 70-71.

Strip cartoons

A strip cartoon is a joke told in more than one frame. Like a single cartoon, the joke needs to be visual. It can be like a short story with a punchline.

One of the hardest things about drawing a strip cartoon is making characters look the same in each frame. To start with, only use one or two characters. Give them features which you find easy to draw.

How to start

Close-ups varied with larger scenes.

As with single cartoons, think of a theme first and make up a joke around it.

Divide the joke up into three or four stages. You can vary the sizes of the frames, and close-ups with larger scenes, to make the strip look more interesting.

Speech bubbles

SMOOTH!

Thinks...

WHISPER

EEK!

CURVY

FRILLY!

Put bubbles over background areas with no detail.

You can put speech and thoughts in bubbles in the pictures. These can be different shapes. The shape of the bubble may suggest the way something is being said.

Keep the speech short or the strip gets complicated and the bubbles take up too much room. Make sure you allow room for bubbles when you sketch out the pictures.

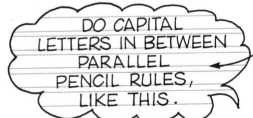

DO CAPITAL LETTERS IN BETWEEN PARALLEL PENCIL RULES, LIKE THIS.

Pencil rules

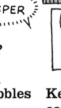

MAKE EACH LINE ROUGHLY THE SAME LENGTH. CENTRE THEM BY DRAWING A VERTICAL RULE AND PUTTING THE SAME NUMBER OF LETTERS EITHER SIDE OF THE RULE ON EACH LINE.

It is best to do the lettering before you draw the bubble outline. Use a pen with a fine tip.

To get the letters the same height, draw parallel pencil rules and letter in between them, as above. Then rub out the pencil lines. The letters are likely to be quite small, so it is best to use capital letters which are easier to read.

A finished strip

This strip is about a caveman. He is quite an easy character to repeat from frame to frame because of his simple features and clothing.*

Speech bubble over the sky area.

Different sized frames make strip more interesting.

Sound effects make the strip more fun. As you read it you imagine the noises so it is a bit like watching a film.

Bright colours make the characters stand out. The background is paler.

A lot of the humour in a strip cartoon comes from the expressions on the characters faces.

When positioning speech bubbles, remember that people read from left to right down the frame. They will read bubbles at the top before they read bubbles further down.

Borders for the strip

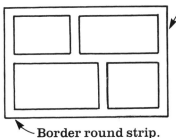

Border round strip.

Use a ruler and a pen with a slightly thicker tip than the one you used for the lettering. You can put the whole strip in a larger box.

Freehand borders are finished off without a ruler.

1. Place a ruler just below where you want to draw the line.

2. Run your fingers along the ruler as you paint. (You may need to practise this.)

The borders round the frames can make a strip look neat and tidy or free and artistic. Here are some ideas for different borders.

Freehand borders give a sketchy effect. To keep them straight, draw the lines in pencil with a ruler. Then go over them in ink.

Paintbrush borders are nice because the line varies slightly in thickness. You can get a straight line using the method above.

*You can find out how to draw dinosaurs on pages 46-47.

Comic strips

You may have your own favourite comics. The stories in them are fun to read because there is very little text and a lot of action in the pictures.

These two pages describe how a comic strip artist creates a comic strip. You could try making up your own comic strip in the same way.

Creating a comic strip

A practical joke . . . an escape from the zoo . . . an arctic expedition . . . a kidnap!

The first thing to do when creating a comic strip is to think of a plot. It needs to be funny or dramatic – or both. The plot needs an exciting finish.

Bad-tempered.

Tough and reliable.

Lively and clever.

Grumbling and lazy.

The characters need strong personalities which will come across in the pictures. You can tell what the characters above are like just from looking at them.

Find out how to use special effects to add excitement to your pictures on pages 28-29.

The plot needs to be full of action to keep the reader interested. The story needs to move fast and something new must happen in each picture.

Writing a script

A script explains what is happening in each frame of the comic strip. It describes the scenery, what the characters are doing and saying and any sound effects. Some artists write their own scripts. Others illustrate scripts written by someone else.

The page of a comic is a fixed size so the story needs to be divided up into the right number of frames to fit on it.

```
SCRIPT: THE TESTTUBE AFFAIR            PAGE 1

Frame 1.
Scene: room furnished with an iron bedstead.
There is a small window. Terry is sitting
tied to a chair, busy freeing himself.

Thought bubble: Whoever heard of a kidnapper
who couldn't tie knots? I've been lucky.

Frame 2.
Scene: Sparsely-furnished room. There is a
radio on the table. Two mean and
grubby-looking kidnappers sit playing cards.

First kidnapper: Why do we always get the
boring jobs?
Second kidnapper: Shuddup and listen!

Frame 3.
Close-up of radio blaring: The kidnappers of
Terry Testtube, son of Professor Testtube the
famous scientist, are still at large. Today
the Professor made an appeal, saying that he
would disclose his new wonder invention if
the kidnappers would return his son.

Frame 4.
Scene: Back to room where Terry is
imprisoned. He has tied a rope to the leg of
the bedstead and is sitting the other side of
the door ready to pull it tight. He is about
to lob half a brick through the window.

Terry: This ought to fool those two idiots.
```

Drawing the strip

Here you can see how the script on the left (you can only see the first page) was made into a finished comic strip. It was drawn using a dip pen with a sprung nib. The nib gives a varying thickness of line depending on how hard it is pressed.

The story is mainly told in the pictures but there are bubbles for speech and thoughts.

Pressure on nib gives a thick line.

Frame sizes are varied to make strip more interesting.

A line of text at the top can explain changes of scene or time lapses.

Some frames can be left without borders to add variety.

Light pressure on nib gives a finer line.

This is a freeze-frame picture (see page 15).

Scenery can make the strip come to life.

Special effects

Special effects can make cartoons look exciting. Here are some ideas for how to add drama and atmosphere to your pictures. You can make them spooky, mysterious, shocking or scary. You can also find out how to add sound effects.

Sound effects

You can add sound effects by using words and shapes which suggest the sound. The most common ones are explosions but there are lots of others you can use.

Jagged speech bubble suggests shock.

Silhouette of a castle in a thunderstorm.

Shadows and silhouettes

Using different lighting effects for night pictures can make them look creepy or mysterious. Here are some suggestions:

Huge shadow on wall.

Silhouettes in a lighted window. These are made by people sitting in front of a source of light.

28

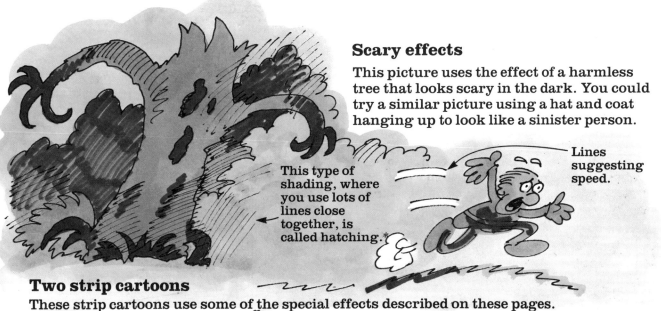

Scary effects

This picture uses the effect of a harmless tree that looks scary in the dark. You could try a similar picture using a hat and coat hanging up to look like a sinister person.

This type of shading, where you use lots of lines close together, is called hatching.*

Lines suggesting speed.

Two strip cartoons

These strip cartoons use some of the special effects described on these pages.

1

MIIIAAAOOOW!

BOOM!

BANK MANAGER'S LUNCH BOX

2

CLOMP! CLOMP!

CLOMP! CLOMP!

A strip cartoon to try

Here is a script for a strip cartoon involving special effects for you to try.
Frame 1: Silhouettes of people by a bonfire.
Frame 2: Boy dressed up as a ghost frightens them away.

Frame 3: Boy takes sheet off and is shocked to hear laughter coming from a spooky tree silhouette.
Sound effect: HO HO HO

*You can find out about other ways to shade on page 71.

Cartoon story books

Cartoon stories are like long comic strips. The story is told in pictures with lots of action and excitement.

Tintin is one of the best known cartoon story characters. He and his dog, Snowy, first appeared in 1929 as a comic strip serial in a weekly children's newspaper. Later, the stories were made into magazines and books.

Who created Tintin?

Tintin

Captain Haddock

Snowy

Professor Calculus

Characters in the Tintin stories.*

One of the identical twin detectives, Thomson and Thompson.

A Belgian man called Hergé created Tintin. Hergé's real name was Georges Remi. The name Hergé came from the French pronunciation of his initials, G.R., backwards. He was born in 1907 and died in 1983.

The Studios Hergé

Until the early 1940s, Hergé worked alone on Tintin. Later he assembled a team to help colour in the pictures, letter the speech bubbles and so on. This team became known as the Studios Hergé. All the stories were thoroughly researched so that details of costume, architecture, machinery and so on were correct.

The ship Unicorn, from *The Secret of the Unicorn* and *Red Rackham's Treasure* was based on ships in the French navy in the 17th century.*

The Inca masks in this picture from *Prisoners of the Sun*, were based on the sketch on the right.*

Sketch by a 19th century explorer of Peru and Bolivia.

First Hergé wrote a plot and sketched the drawings. He then worked on the drawings, redrawing them as many as ten times. The drawings were then handed to his assistants. They filled in backgrounds, coloured the pictures and drew and lettered the speech bubbles. Hergé drew all the characters and checked the final pictures.

*Drawings by Hergé. © Studios Hergé/Casterman Publishers

Hergé's techniques

The Tintin books have a very distinctive style. Here you can see some of its features in a section from *Prisoners of the Sun*. Many of them add variety to the picture strips so that they look lively, exciting and never boring.*

Unusual angles look dramatic and make the story more interesting.
▼

The pictures are clear and the outlines are unbroken.
▼

Hergé varied the sizes of frames to add variety and suit the picture.
▼

The faces show many different expressions.
▼

Colours are clear and flat with no shading.
▼

▲
Costumes and scenery were thoroughly researched so that all details were correct.

▲
Background colours are plain and muted. The bright costumes stand out against them.

▲
Hergé varied close-ups with larger pictures of single characters and scenes with lots of people.

The stories are full of suspense and drama. This is because they were first published in newspaper serials. Hergé needed to create suspense at the end of each instalment.

*Drawings by Hergé. © Studios Hergé/Casterman Publishers

Drawing animals

You can draw animals in a similar way to drawing people, by using simple shapes and lines and adding features.

Animals make good cartoons because you can use their natural characteristics, such as claws, tails, ears and so on to give them personality. Here are lots of animals to draw.*

Cat

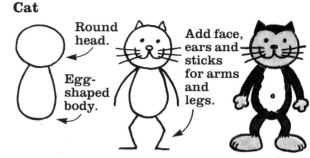

Round head.

Egg-shaped body.

Add face, ears and sticks for arms and legs.

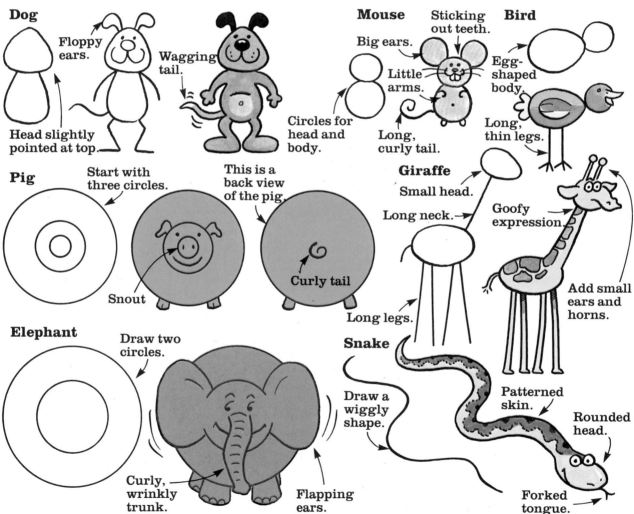

Dog

Floppy ears.

Wagging tail.

Head slightly pointed at top.

Mouse

Big ears.

Sticking out teeth.

Little arms.

Circles for head and body.

Long, curly tail.

Bird

Egg-shaped body.

Long, thin legs.

Pig

Start with three circles.

This is a back view of the pig.

Snout

Curly tail

Giraffe

Small head.

Long neck.

Goofy expression.

Long legs.

Add small ears and horns.

Elephant

Draw two circles.

Curly, wrinkly trunk.

Flapping ears.

Snake

Draw a wiggly shape.

Patterned skin.

Rounded head.

Forked tongue.

Lion

Body shape is similar to dog.

Eyebrows raised in a superior expression.

Curly mane.

Snout

Large paws.

Fish

Round eyes.

Gaping mouth.

Tropical fish.

Monkey

Sticking out ears.

Long arms.

Similar body shape to cat with snout.

Thin legs.

Long tail.

Whale

Rounded fish shape.

Water spout.

Cow

Triangular-shaped head.

Oblong-shaped body.

Horns and ears.

Udder

Sheep

Large body.

Small head.

Silly expression.

Woolly fleece.

Thin legs.

Animals in cartoons

Cartoons may look very violent but usually no real harm is done. The cartoon below might help you think up a few of your own animal cartoons.

SPLAT!

33

How cartoon films are made

The most famous cartoon film maker in the world was Walt Disney. He made such films as Mickey Mouse and Bambi. He started work in the 1920s. Although equipment and materials have improved over the years, the way cartoon films are made has changed very little.

On the next four pages you can find out how cartoon films are made. This is called cartoon animation.

How film works

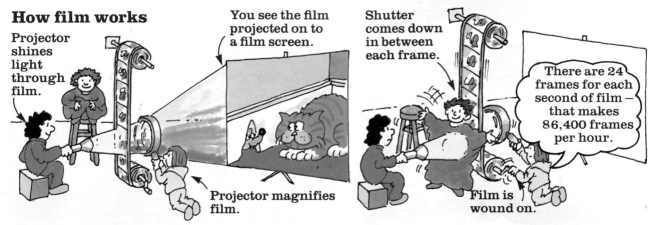

Projector shines light through film.

You see the film projected on to a film screen.

Projector magnifies film.

Shutter comes down in between each frame.

There are 24 frames for each second of film — that makes 86,400 frames per hour.

Film is wound on.

A film is a sequence of tiny pictures, or frames. There are 24 frames for each second of film. A projector shines light through them and magnifies them.

Each frame is held still in front of the projector just long enough for you to see it. Then a shutter comes down while the next frame is positioned.

This happens so fast that you do not notice individual frames or the shutter. Without the shutter between frames, the film would look like a long blur.

Making the film

A cartoon film is made by taking photos of thousands of drawings. The drawings show all the different stages of movement.

The photos of the drawings are combined into a film strip. (There is more about how all this is done over the page.)

Each photo makes one frame. 24 frames make one second of the film. Below, you can see the frames in one second of a film.

24 frames make one second of film.

Planning the film

The story of the film is divided up into scenes. The artists working on the film, called the animators, do a set of drawings. This shows what happens in each scene. It is called a storyboard.

The storyboard is a bit like a strip cartoon. What the characters are saying is written under the pictures.

Storyboard

Animating the film

The animators break each scene down into different movements. Then, each animator works on drawing one movement at a time: for instance, a sneeze.

The animator draws the start and end of the sneeze and a few of the main stages in between.

These pictures are called key pictures. Each key picture is numbered. The numbers show how many other stages need to be drawn in between to complete the sneeze.

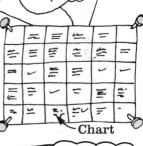

Key pictures

The animator has a chart showing what will happen during each split second of the film — action, speech, sound effects and music. The movements drawn are matched to the sound.

Chart

Look over the page to see what happens next.

35

Completing the drawings

Key picture

In-betweener adds these pictures.

Key picture

Once all the key pictures have been drawn, they are passed on to other members of the animating team.

These members are called in-betweeners because they do the drawings in between the key pictures.

The numbers on the key pictures show the in-betweener how many more pictures are needed.

How the artists work

Each animator or in-betweener works on a flat box with a glass surface, called a light box.

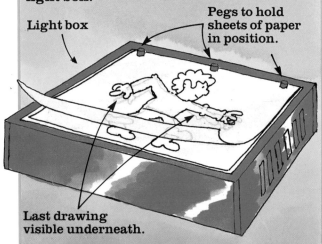

Light box

Pegs to hold sheets of paper in position.

Last drawing visible underneath.

Light shining up through the glass means the artist can put several pieces of paper on top of each other, and still see the shapes on the papers underneath. The artist can trace the character, except for parts that are meant to move.

Tracing and colouring

The finished drawings are traced on to transparent sheets called cels.

Each cel is then turned over and painted on the back, so that brush strokes do not show on the front. The cels are now ready for the next stage, when they are photographed. This stage is called shooting.

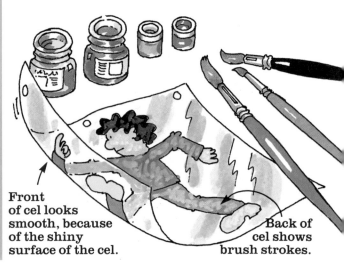

Front of cel looks smooth, because of the shiny surface of the cel.

Back of cel shows brush strokes.

Background scenery

Background scenery is painted on long rolls of paper. During shooting, the scenery is laid on the plate of a rostrum camera (see right). The cel with the character drawn on it is placed on top of it.

Background scenery

Cel with character drawn on it.

Each time a new cel is put on the plate, the background scenery can be moved to either side. This makes it look as if the character is moving.

Background scenery rolls this way.

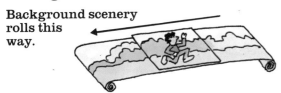

The character stays in the same place on the plate of the camera, but the scenery is moved behind him. This makes it look as if he is running along.

Rostrum camera

The type of camera used to take photographs for a cartoon film is called a rostrum camera. One cel at a time is placed on the plate of the camera and a picture taken. All the photos are combined into one reel of film.

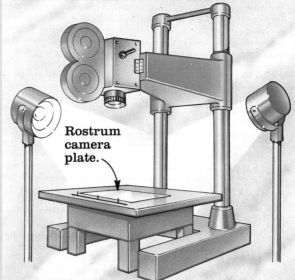

Rostrum camera plate.

Flick the pages and watch your cartoon say hello.

Animate your own cartoon

Use a small notebook with thin paper so you can see the line of a black felt tip pen through the page.

Hold the notebook firmly closed. Draw three thick, black lines across the tops of all the pages.

On the first page, copy the picture above. Tear it out. Number the next ten pages from one to ten.

Trace your picture on to pages one and ten. Use the marks at the top of the page to line the pages up.

On page five, trace the head, but make him raise his hat. You now have three key pictures.

Draw the in-between stages. Start with page nine and work back. Trace parts staying still.

Mix and match

Here are lots of pictures of heads, bodies and legs from different sides. You can copy them and use them in your own pictures. Remember that a person's head might be facing you while the body is sideways on, and vice versa.

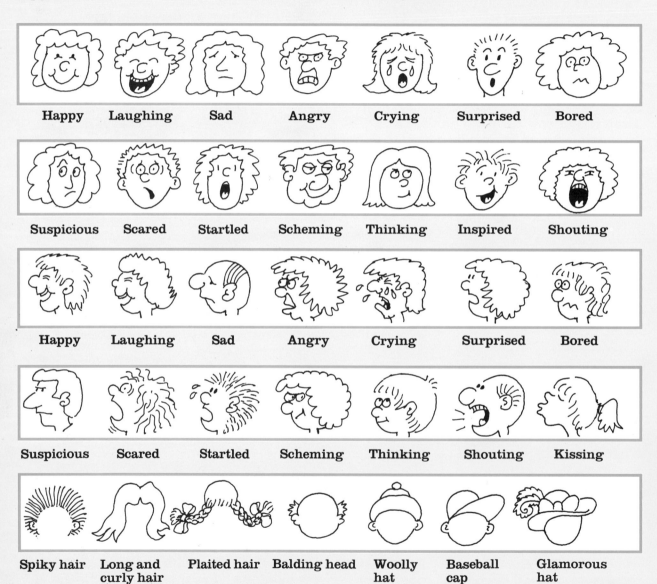

| Happy | Laughing | Sad | Angry | Crying | Surprised | Bored |

| Suspicious | Scared | Startled | Scheming | Thinking | Inspired | Shouting |

| Happy | Laughing | Sad | Angry | Crying | Surprised | Bored |

| Suspicious | Scared | Startled | Scheming | Thinking | Shouting | Kissing |

| Spiky hair | Long and curly hair | Plaited hair | Balding head | Woolly hat | Baseball cap | Glamorous hat |

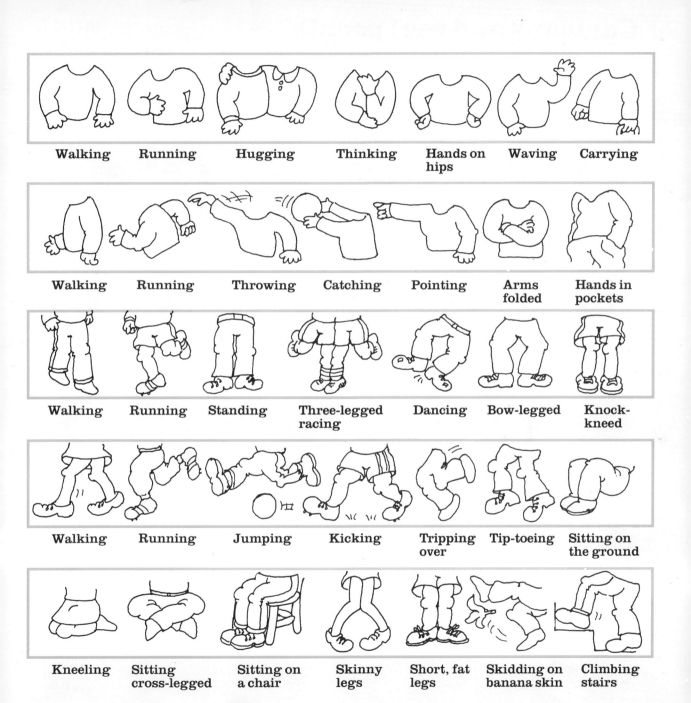

Walking Running Hugging Thinking Hands on hips Waving Carrying

Walking Running Throwing Catching Pointing Arms folded Hands in pockets

Walking Running Standing Three-legged racing Dancing Bow-legged Knock-kneed

Walking Running Jumping Kicking Tripping over Tip-toeing Sitting on the ground

Kneeling Sitting cross-legged Sitting on a chair Skinny legs Short, fat legs Skidding on banana skin Climbing stairs

Cartoons and real people

Cartoons look friendly and funny. They have big heads, hands and feet and you can easily give them funny expressions. They have a cuddly, rounded shape. The rules for drawing real people are different, as you can see on this page.

Heads

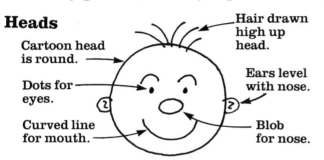

Cartoon head is round. →

Hair drawn high up head.

Dots for eyes. →

Ears level with nose.

Curved line for mouth. →

Blob for nose.

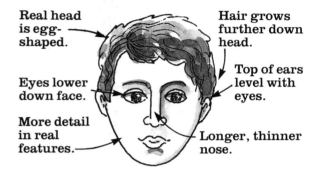

Real head is egg-shaped.

Hair grows further down head.

Eyes lower down face.

Top of ears level with eyes.

More detail in real features.

Longer, thinner nose.

A cartoon nose goes in the middle of the face. A real nose is long rather than blob-shaped and the nostrils are low down the face.

Real eyes are lower down the face than cartoon eyes. Cartoon ears are level with the nose. Real ears are more level with the eyes.

Cartoon features are simple and you do not need to shade cartoon heads. They usually look quite flat. You shade a real head to give it shape.

Bodies

The proportions of cartoon people are different to those of real people. A whole cartoon body is about four times as long as its head. A real body is seven or eight times as long as its head.

Hands and feet are usually bigger on a cartoon and the body shape is more rounded. Look at the differences on the right.

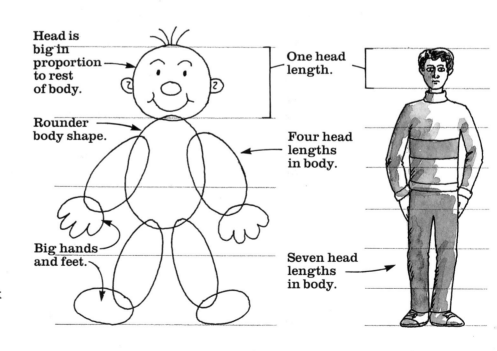

Head is big in proportion to rest of body.

Rounder body shape.

Big hands and feet.

One head length.

Four head lengths in body.

Seven head lengths in body.

Part 2
HOW TO DRAW
MONSTERS
AND OTHER CREATURES
Cheryl Evans

Designed and illustrated by Graham Round and Kim Blundell

Additional design and illustration by Brian Robertson

Contents

42	About part two
43	Getting ideas
44	Monster shapes
46	Drawing dinosaurs
48	Spooky monsters
50	Space aliens
52	Sea monsters
54	Man-made monsters
56	Dragons

58	Giants, ogres and trolls
60	Goblins, dwarfs and human horrors
62	Mythical creatures
64	Animal monsters
66	People or monsters?
68	Mechanical monsters
70	Techniques and materials
72	Index

Consultant: Jocelyn Clarke

About part two

Monsters come in all shapes and sizes. They can be quite simple or fairly tricky to draw. This part of the book shows you how to draw lots of different monsters and colour them to make them look really dramatic.

Shapes to use.

Monster shapes
There are some ideas for monster shapes to start you drawing on pages 44-45.

Dinosaur

Famous monsters

King Kong

Some of the most famous monsters in the world are here, too. Try drawing the Minotaur (page 63) or King Kong (page 65).

All kinds of monsters
There are all kinds of monsters. For example, there are dinosaurs on pages 46-47, space aliens on pages 50-51, and giants on pages 58-59.

Fuzzy alien

Vac-dragon

Unusual monsters
You can turn anything into a monster. Try a vacuum cleaner (page 54), a blob (page 51) or a computer (page 69).

Scary settings
Scenery can make your monsters more exciting. See how to do a watery background for sea monsters on page 53, or a spooky graveyard on page 49, for instance.

Things to use
In this part of the book, you will see how to use pencils, felt-tips, crayons, chalk and other materials. There is a chart at the back to remind you of all the different things you can do.

Getting ideas

Some of the best monsters come from your own imagination. On this page there are pictures of the kinds of things that can inspire you. You will find ways to use ideas like these later in the book.

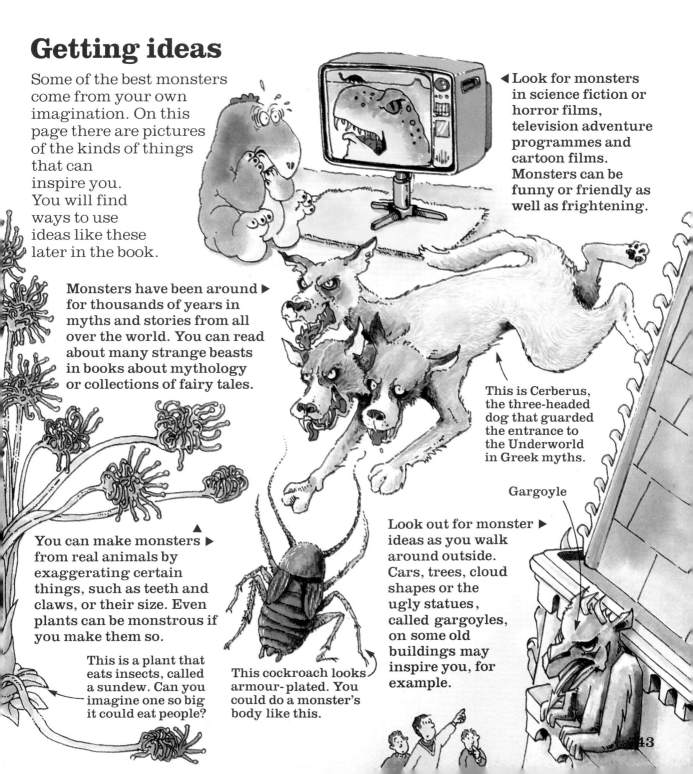

◀ Look for monsters in science fiction or horror films, television adventure programmes and cartoon films. Monsters can be funny or friendly as well as frightening.

Monsters have been around ▶ for thousands of years in myths and stories from all over the world. You can read about many strange beasts in books about mythology or collections of fairy tales.

This is Cerberus, the three-headed dog that guarded the entrance to the Underworld in Greek myths.

Gargoyle

You can make monsters ▶ from real animals by exaggerating certain things, such as teeth and claws, or their size. Even plants can be monstrous if you make them so.

This is a plant that eats insects, called a sundew. Can you imagine one so big it could eat people?

This cockroach looks armour-plated. You could do a monster's body like this.

Look out for monster ▶ ideas as you walk around outside. Cars, trees, cloud shapes or the ugly statues, called gargoyles, on some old buildings may inspire you, for example.

Monster shapes

Here are some ideas for monster shapes. Find out below how the shape of a monster can make it look frightening or friendly or make your skin crawl.

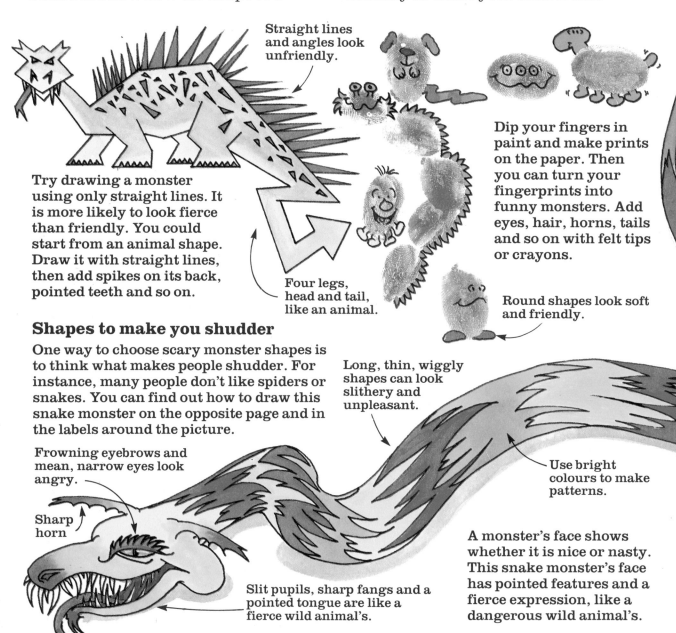

Straight lines and angles look unfriendly.

Try drawing a monster using only straight lines. It is more likely to look fierce than friendly. You could start from an animal shape. Draw it with straight lines, then add spikes on its back, pointed teeth and so on.

Four legs, head and tail, like an animal.

Dip your fingers in paint and make prints on the paper. Then you can turn your fingerprints into funny monsters. Add eyes, hair, horns, tails and so on with felt tips or crayons.

Round shapes look soft and friendly.

Shapes to make you shudder

One way to choose scary monster shapes is to think what makes people shudder. For instance, many people don't like spiders or snakes. You can find out how to draw this snake monster on the opposite page and in the labels around the picture.

Long, thin, wiggly shapes can look slithery and unpleasant.

Frowning eyebrows and mean, narrow eyes look angry.

Sharp horn

Use bright colours to make patterns.

Slit pupils, sharp fangs and a pointed tongue are like a fierce wild animal's.

A monster's face shows whether it is nice or nasty. This snake monster's face has pointed features and a fierce expression, like a dangerous wild animal's.

44

Draw a snake monster

Draw a wiggly line. Follow it with another line close to it. Add a pointed tail at one end and a fierce head at the other. Colour it in.

Pointed tail ➔

A friendly monster

Mop of hair looks soft.

Big, round eyes like a baby.

Blunt teeth are not as scary as sharp ones.

Upward-curving mouth makes a smile.

Rounded shapes are friendlier than sharp, spiky ones. This monster's cuddly body, big, round eyes and smiling mouth make it look cheerful and lovable.

Mixed monsters

If you mix shapes it can be hard to tell if the monster is nice or nasty. You could draw some mixed monster shapes of your own, like these ones, and try to decide if they are nice or not.

Round body, but sharp teeth and claws.

Sharp shapes for body, but smiling face.

45

Drawing dinosaurs

Dinosaurs were huge, real-life monsters that existed on Earth 150-200 million years ago. Here you can find out how to draw and colour some of them. You can adapt these basic shapes to make many others.*

Tyrannosaurus rex

Tyrannosaurus rex was the king of the meat-eating dinosaurs. It could grow to nearly 15 metres (49 feet) long. The picture in the box below shows you how to draw it. Hints for colouring and other details are shown on the right.

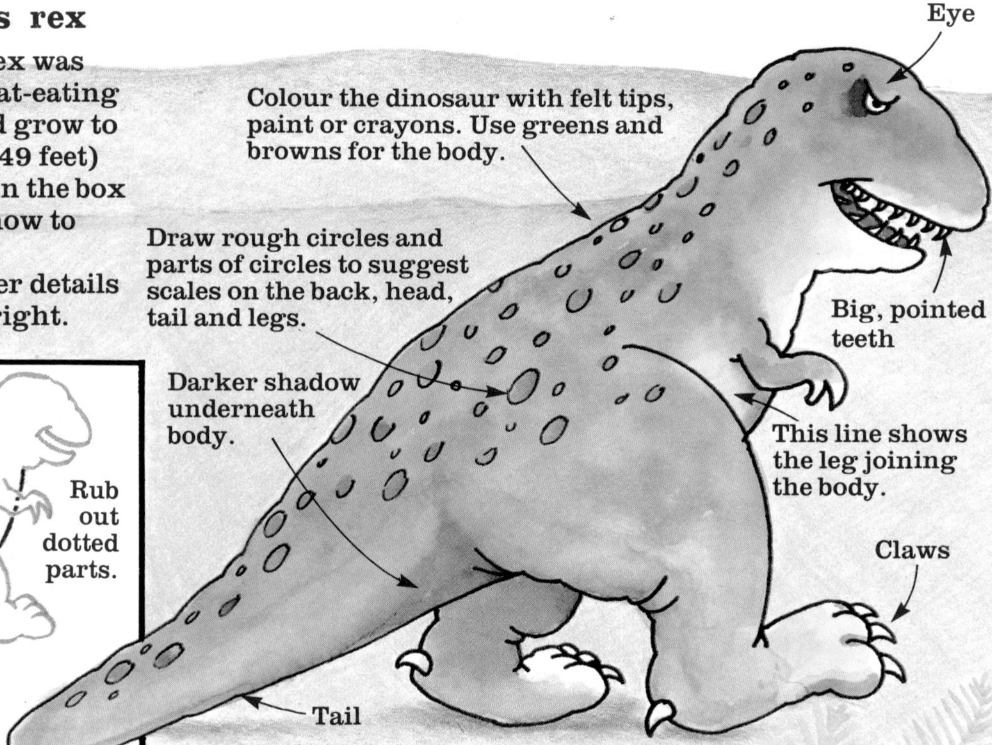

Colour the dinosaur with felt tips, paint or crayons. Use greens and browns for the body.

Draw rough circles and parts of circles to suggest scales on the back, head, tail and legs.

Darker shadow underneath body.

Eye

Big, pointed teeth

This line shows the leg joining the body.

Claws

Tail

Drawing the shape

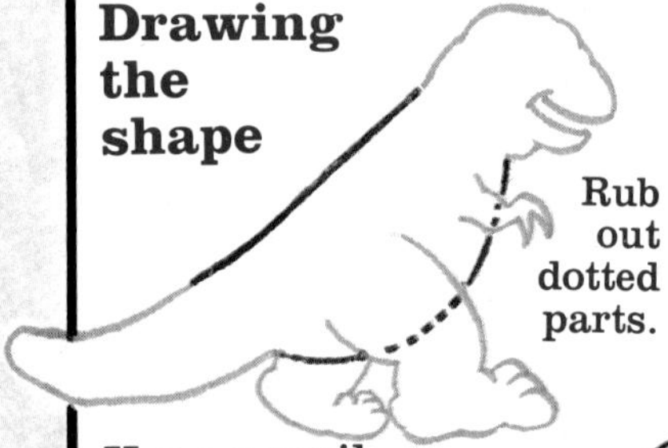

Rub out dotted parts.

Use a pencil to copy the lines shown in the picture in this order:

—— First, the black lines.
—— Next, the orange lines.
—— Then the blue lines.

The boxes on page 47 show you how to draw two more dinosaurs. Copy the lines in the same order – black, then orange, then blue.

Giant fern

During the dinosaur period the Earth was warm and covered in dense forests. Plants were giant-sized, though many of them were like forest plants today.

Try drawing giant ferns, like this one, as a setting for your dinosaurs. Do curved lines for stems. Add narrow leaves on each side. The leaves get shorter towards the tip of each stem.

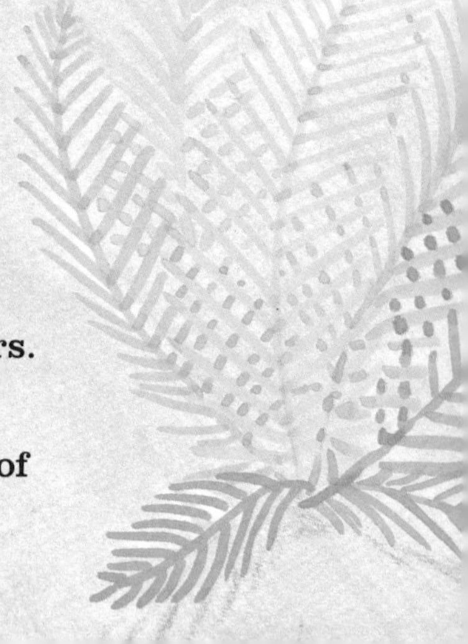

*There is a dinosaur in a strip cartoon on page 25.

Flying monsters

At the same time as the dinosaurs, there were also flying reptiles, like this pterodactyl. Copy the lines in the box below to draw it.

Sharp teeth

Scaly body like tyrannosaurus rex. Use brown paint or felt tip.

Use crayons for the wings (see below). This contrasts well with the body.

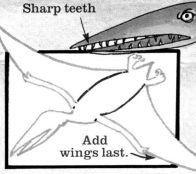

Add wings last.

Wing texture

The pterodactyl has bat-like wings. Get this effect by putting a leaf face-down under the paper and rubbing over it with a brown crayon.

Use a leaf with veins that stick out. A horse-chestnut or maple is good.

Diplodocus

This is a diplodocus. See ▶ how to draw it in the box below.

You can use the diplodocus shape, or any of the shapes on this page, as a base for drawing other monsters.

Use greys for the diplodocus.

Add an eye and a mouth.

Go over darker parts twice.

Put a black shadow underneath the body.

Diplodocus skin

To get a wrinkly skin texture as in this picture, put a sheet of rough sandpaper under your drawing and colour over the top with crayons. Press quite hard. Wax crayons look brighter than pencil crayons.

Spooky monsters

Ghosts are scary because nobody knows exactly what they are or if they even exist. Some people say they are shadowy, almost see-through shapes that appear in the dark. Here are some different kinds for you to try.

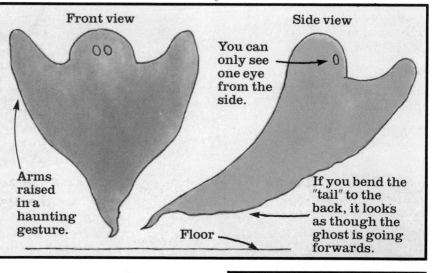

Floating ghost

This floating ghost shape looks a bit like someone with a sheet over their head and arms raised.

Give it a rounded head and wiggly "tail" where its feet would be so it looks as though it is fading away.

Draw the floor below the "tail" so the ghost seems to float.

Front view

Side view

You can only see one eye from the side.

Arms raised in a haunting gesture.

If you bend the "tail" to the back, it looks as though the ghost is going forwards.

Floor

Changing the shape

You can change the shape of a ghost to make it do different things. Give it an expression, too. Try some of the ideas below.

◄ Make a ghost do something normal, like sitting and reading. You can see the chair through the ghost.

◄ Give a furious ghost hands on its hips and an angry face. Do frowning eyebrows and a straight line for a mouth. Red is a good angry colour.

Ghostly colours

Here's one good way to do ghostly colours: draw the outline in felt tip. Then smudge the line with a wet paintbrush and spread the colour inside the shape.

Expressions to try

Why not try some ghostly expressions? Here are some tips to help you.*

Friendly: round eyes, curved eyebrows, and a smile. ▶

Surprised: open mouth, round eyes, raised eyebrows. ▶

Sad: eyebrows and eyes slope, mouth curves down. ▶

There is more about expressions on pages 6-7.

Graveyard phantom

Follow these stages to draw this spooky phantom in an eerie graveyard. It is easier to do than it may look.

1. Make a charcoal patch on white paper with a charcoal pencil or stick.

2. With a rubber, rub out a ghost shape, gravestones and blades of grass.

3. Add details with charcoal as in the picture.

Rubbed out ghost shape.

Charcoal eyes and mouth.

Gravestone rubbed out.

Charcoal shadows.

Grass shapes rubbed out.

Headless spectre

Here is another type of ghost. It is in historical costume and has its head under its arm. To draw one like it, use white chalk on black paper. The instructions below should help.

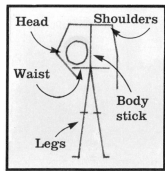

Head

Shoulders

Waist

Body stick

Legs

With a pencil, draw a stick man like this on your paper. Do legs twice as long as the body. Draw the head half as long as the body and to one side. Add lines for waist, shoulders and arms.

Join shoulders and waist. Do neck ruff, bloomers and feet. Add details from the picture on the left. Rub out extra lines. Go over the outline in chalk, then smudge it gently with a finger. *

*Stop further smudging with fixative spray (see page 70).

Space aliens

What do you think aliens from outer space look like? Are they like slightly odd people or completely different?

There are some different kinds of aliens here for you to try and some space backgrounds for them, too.

Little green Martian

1 **2** **3** **4**

1. To draw the Martian, start with rough pencil circles for his head, body and feet.

2 and 3. With your pencil, add the lines shown in red in these two pictures.

4. Rub out unwanted lines. Do the final outline in black and colour him in.

Double space scene

Here's a way to get two dramatic space scenes in one go. You need wax crayons, coloured chalks, a pencil and two sheets of white paper. Just follow the steps below.

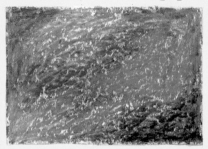

For these pictures you need three layers of colour. Use chalk for the first layer. Cover a sheet of paper with bright patches of chalk as shown here.

Colour over the chalk with a bright wax crayon – orange or yellow, say. Do the third layer with a dark wax crayon such as blue or green. It will look a bit like this.

Lay a second sheet of paper on top of the one you have coloured. Draw stars, planets, space ships or aliens in pencil on the top sheet. Press quite hard.

These blobs have been made into aliens in the scene below.

Moon blobs

Make blob aliens by drawing blob shapes like those above and adding features to them. You and your friends could draw blobs for each other to turn into aliens.

Do an outer space scene by drawing blob monsters on the moon. Paint the moon's mountains and craters white and grey and do a black sky with stars. A good way to spray stars is to dip an old toothbrush in white paint. Hold it bristles-down over the paper and run a finger along the bristles.

Craters have steep sides and a flat top with a hole in it.

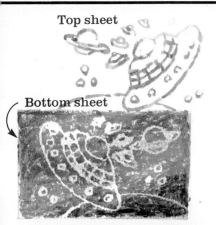

Top sheet

Bottom sheet

Remove the top sheet and turn it over. You now have two pictures. The one on the top sheet is made with wax crayon lifted from the other sheet by the pencil lines.

Friendly, fuzzy alien

This fuzzy alien looks soft and friendly. Use charcoal or a soft pencil to draw it. (Pencils can be hard or soft. Find out more about this on page 30.) This is what you do:

Draw a big nose.

Draw lines back and forwards like this.

Move in a circle round the nose.

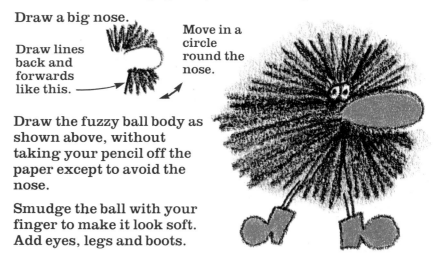

Draw the fuzzy ball body as shown above, without taking your pencil off the paper except to avoid the nose.

Smudge the ball with your finger to make it look soft. Add eyes, legs and boots.

Sea monsters

These monsters are all based on things that live in the sea. Find out how to draw them, colour them and do a watery background below.

You can see half a head and one evil red eye.

Giant octopus

This giant octopus is splashing in a cloud of its own dark ink so you cannot see how big it is or where all its tentacles are. Perhaps one of them is reaching out to grab you?

Tentacles twist and curl.

Suckers.

Add white stripes if you like.

How to draw it

1. Draw the whole octopus lightly in pencil. It has a blobby head and eight coiling tentacles.

2. Mix black and blue paint and, with a brush, splash it on and around the monster, hiding parts of it.

3. When the splashes dry, paint the bits of octopus you can still see black. Add details as shown above.

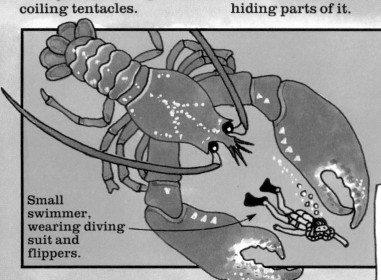

Small swimmer, wearing diving suit and flippers.

Supersized sea creatures

Everyone knows that lobsters are smaller than people. But see what happens if you draw them the other way round, as here.

There are some more small sea creature shapes below. Try doing similar pictures using them.

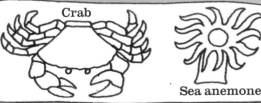

Crab

Sea anemone

Fantastic fish

Invent a fantastic fish monster by drawing a big fish shape like this, with a huge mouth, sharp teeth, bulbous eyes and so on. Find out how to give it a slimy fish skin below.

Staring eyes

Spiky fins and tail.

Sharp teeth

Sharp shapes are scary.

Slimy fish skin

To do a slimy fish skin, first paint your fish with water or very watery colour. While it is still very wet, dab on blobs of bright paint. The blobs will smudge and blot to give mottled markings. Paint eyes and other details when the fish is dry.

Sea serpent

This sea serpent in the seaweed is coloured with wax crayons. If you use them to do an underwater scene, you can put a water wash (see right) on top afterwards because water and wax don't mix.

Water wash

To do a water wash background as on this page, paint clean water all over your paper with a thick paintbrush. While it is still very wet, add watery blue and green paint in streaks. Let them mix and merge. Tape all four edges of the paper on to a flat surface while it dries to stop it wrinkling.

Drawing the serpent

Draw a wiggly serpent in pencil.* With wax crayon, add fronds of weed. Make some go over the serpent's body and some go behind it. Colour the serpent with wax crayons, except where the weeds go over its body.

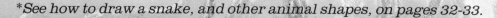

*See how to draw a snake, and other animal shapes, on pages 32-33.

Man-made monsters

If you can imagine things like a machine coming alive or a bad-tempered house, you can make monsters out of almost anything. Making something that is not alive look as if it can think or move is called anthropomorphism. See how to do it here.

Household horrors

Imagine household objects coming alive and doing things of their own accord. They may be nice, but you can make them horrible, like this cooker and vacuum cleaner.

Crazy cooker

In the box on the right is an ordinary cooker shape. On the far side of it you can see one that has been made into a cooker monster.

Vac-dragon

This vacuum cleaner turns into a dragon with a snaky neck. The sucking part becomes a head with a wide mouth. Just add two evil eyes and feet with claws.

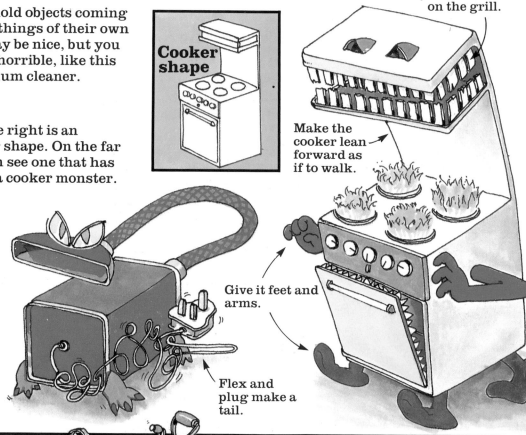

Cooker shape

Put eyes and teeth on the grill.

Make the cooker lean forward as if to walk.

Give it feet and arms.

Flex and plug make a tail.

Kitchen shapes

Scissors

Cheese grater

Egg whisk

Here are some kitchen shapes to turn into monsters. Copy them and add eyes, arms, legs and teeth as you like.

Mean streets

On a dark night, in a badly lit street, a row of houses can look menacing.* Windows turn into eyes and doors look like mouths. On the left is a particularly horrid row. The shapes are quite simple so you could try drawing your own.

Dark doors look like open mouths.

Bottles on step look like teeth.

Reflections in windows make eyes.

Shadow spider plant

Shadows can easily become monsters. See how the plant below casts a horrible spidery shadow.*

Try it yourself. Put a plant on a table by a wall in a dark room. Shine a torch or lamp on it to make a shadow on the wall. Different plants will make different shapes.

To draw it, first do the plant and pot and colour them. Behind, put a patch of yellow and then smudge charcoal around the edges. Add the big black shadow.

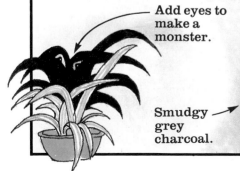

Add eyes to make a monster.

Smudgy grey charcoal.

Convertible car

Here are four steps to help you convert an ordinary car into a monstrous-looking beast.

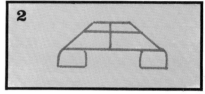

Draw one line down with three lines across it (at top, bottom and a third of the way down). Each line across is twice as long as the line above and is cut in half by the down line.

Join the ends of the lines. Do two squares for the headlights below the bottom line.

4 Adapt the shape to make your car look alive. Use curved lines. Make the lights into eyes with slit pupils. Turn the grille into fangs.

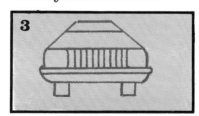

For a bumper do three lines right across below the lights. The wheels are squares below the bumper. Do lines for the grille between the lights.

See pages 28-29 and 67 for more eerie light effects.

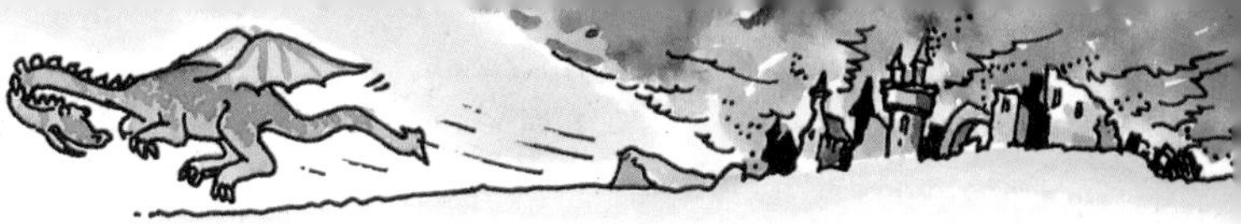

Dragons

Dragons are legendary monsters that lurk in dungeons and caves. They can be friendly but many are dangerous. Here are some dragons to draw.

Fairytale dragon

Most dragons have scaly skin, wings and evil teeth and claws. Follow boxes 1 to 4 to draw a dragon. You can see how to colour it at the bottom of the page.*

1 Head and neck

Copy the picture on the left to draw the head, neck and bulging eye. Then add nostrils, the other eye and spines down the neck as shown.

2 Body and legs

Draw lines for the top and bottom of the body. Add the legs. Rub out the bits shown dotted above.

3 Wing

Draw a fan shaped wing, like in the picture. It looks like part of an umbrella, with spokes going from the bottom up to the point at the top.

Eye sockets

Nostrils

Put darker fingerprints for scales on top of the body colour.

See how to colour the tail to show how it coils.

Add fiery breath, if you like.

Claws

4 Tail

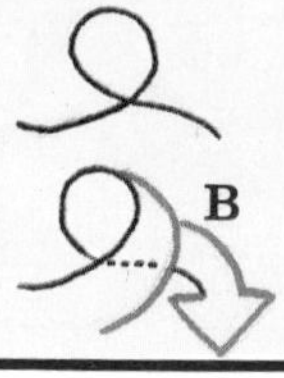

A

B

Add the tail to the back of the body. Join line A to the top of the body and line B (shown in red on the left) to the underneath. Rub out the dotted part.

Painting ideas

Body: green
Scales: when the body is dry add darker fingerprints.
Teeth and claws: yellow.

Wings: pale yellow-green. Do the outline and spokes in dark green.
Mouth and eye: red
Nostril: black

56 *Or use one of the ideas for colouring dinosaurs on pages 46-47.

A dragon's lair

To make a dragon that shines in a dark lair like this one, use coloured chalks on black paper.

First draw the dragon's body. Add wings, claws, eyes and so on in contrasting colours.

For the fiery breath, draw wavy chalk lines and smudge them with a finger.

Do rocky walls in yellow. Smudge red and yellow on them to show how they are lit by the flames.

Make heaps of treasure with splodges of orange, red, green and blue.

Glowing dragon

Here is a way to make dragons that seem to glow in the dark. You need wax crayons, white paper and something pointed, like a knitting needle. Follow these steps.

1. Colour patches of bright wax crayon. Cover them with a thick layer of black crayon, as above.

2. Scratch a dragon's head into the black wax with a knitting needle*. Bright colours will glow through.

3. Your monster will shine in the blackness, like this.

*Be very careful with pointed things.

Giants, ogres and trolls

There are giants in stories from around the world. They are scary because they are so huge. Try some of the tricks shown here to help you draw them.

How to draw a giant

A whole giant is about seven times the length of his head. The circles next to this giant are the size of his head, so you can see how many head lengths different parts of his body are.

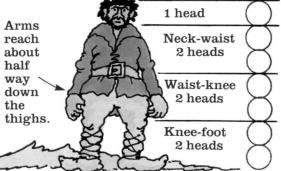

Arms reach about half way down the thighs.

1 head	○
Neck-waist 2 heads	○ ○
Waist-knee 2 heads	○ ○
Knee-foot 2 heads	○ ○

You can draw people in the same way. They are seven times their head length, too. Children only measure about five of their head lengths, though.

How to make a giant look big

To show how big a giant is, put things in the picture to compare him with. In the picture below, compare the giant to the man, his dog and the trees.

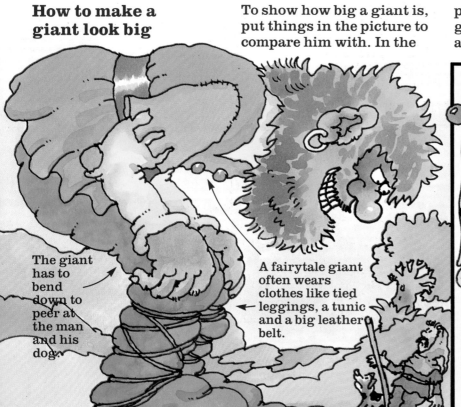

The giant has to bend down to peer at the man and his dog.

A fairytale giant often wears clothes like tied leggings, a tunic and a big leather belt.

Spying giant

Draw a giant spying into a house through the window. You can tell how big he is because his face takes up nearly the whole window frame.

When ogres look small

Castle is far away so it is drawn small.

The ogre is nearly as tall as the tree next to him.

The boy only comes a little way up the tree by him.

The bird is drawn big as it is nearest you.

In this picture the boy is drawn as big as the ogre because he is nearer to you. Near things look bigger than things far away.

In the same way, the trees nearer to you are drawn bigger than those in the distance.

Compare each figure to the tree next to it to judge its true size.

The way things seem to get smaller in the distance is called perspective. You can use it to make pictures look realistic.

Looking up at a troll

If you were standing at the feet of an enormous troll, looking up, he would look a bit like this.

Ask a grown up if you can lie on the floor and look up at them to see for yourself. Their feet look huge, while the rest of their body and head seem small.

The way the parts furthest from you look squashed up and the nearest parts seem to spread out wide is called foreshortening.*

See the hints around the picture for how to draw a troll from down below.

Make the legs and body smaller as they go up.

Do a small head with squashed up features.

His hands look big because they are nearer to you.

Draw enormous feet nearest you.

*Find out more about foreshortening on page 11.

Goblins, dwarfs and human horrors

All the creatures on these two pages have a head, two arms and two legs, like people. But these are supernatural beings that live underground, fly at night, or haunt dark dungeons.

Skeleton

This is a spooky human skeleton. It has been drawn simpler than a real skeleton, which has hundreds of bones and is very hard to draw. Follow the instructions round the picture to help you draw one yourself.

Dwarfs

Dwarfs have short bodies and legs, but big heads, hands and feet. They are usually tubby, with bushy beards.

The dwarfs in this picture are in their forge. They are quite tricky to draw. You could trace them, then try to colour them yourself.*

For a skull, first draw the dome of the head and eye sockets.

Add the teeth and jaw.

Colour the eye sockets black and add a hole for the nose.

The spine is lots of small bones. Draw them close but not touching.

Ribs curve and get shorter near the waist.

This is the pelvis bone. It joins the spine and legs.

Legs and arms have two long, narrow bones each. See how they join at the elbows and knees.

Use pale grey and yellow to colour the skeleton.

Feet and hands have lots of small bones.

Hammer

Faces and fronts lit by flames.

Colours get darker away from the fire.

Tongs

Bellows

Anvil

*See how to mix colours on page 70.

Witch's silhouette

To get the witch's shape, follow these steps.

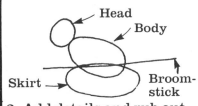

1 Draw these shapes.

Head
Body
Skirt
Broom-stick

2 Add details and rub out extra lines.

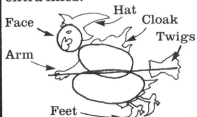

Face
Hat
Cloak
Twigs
Arm
Feet

Paint the witch black.

Draw a circle round her for the moon.

Paint outside the circle black for the night sky.

Tunnel disappears into darkness here.

Draw shoulders jutting from the side of its head so it looks as if its head is sunk low.

Do arms reaching below knees.

Drawing goblins

To draw a goblin, do a thin human shape. Give it knobbly knees and elbows and long, skinny arms. Make its head narrow with pointed ears. Colour it green with glowing eyes.

Try drawing this advancing horde of goblins in a tunnel. Put big goblins at the front of your picture and smaller ones behind. Make the tunnel floor get narrower in the distance and the walls get closer in. This is using perspective (see pages 20-21 and 59 for more about this).

Mythical creatures

Myths from all over the world are full of strange creatures. You may already know some of the ones shown here. Have a go at drawing them using the techniques described.

Mermaid

Mermaids are half woman and half fish. They are lovely, but dangerous. They lure sailors to wreck their ships on rocks.

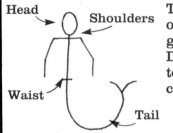

To help you draw one, do a pencil guide, like this. Do a straight line to the waist and a curved line below.

Working round the guide, draw a woman's body to the waist and a fish's tail below. Rub out unwanted lines.

Long hair

Tail

Scales on tail.

Place your mermaid on a rock in the sea and colour her like this.

Medusa

Medusa was a Greek monster. She had snakes instead of hair and anyone that looked at her was turned to stone. To draw her, first draw a horrible face. Then add snaky hair. Try printing snakes with string like this:

1. Cut some pieces of string, as long as you want the snakes to be.

2. Dip them in ink or paint and lay them in coils around the face.

3. Put a piece of scrap paper on top and press with your hand.

4. Remove the scrap paper and pick up the string. Repeat to make more prints.

5. Add eyes and forked tongues at the ends of the snaky hair.

Minotaur

The Minotaur was an Ancient Greek monster with a man's body but the head and shoulders of a giant bull. Here's how you can draw him like a Greek vase painting.

Copy or trace this shape in pencil.

Cover the shape, and the rest of the paper, with orange wax crayon. The shape will still show through.

Paint black inside the shape on top of the orange. Use thick poster paint or mix powder paint and glue.*

When it is dry, scrape markings in the black with a knitting needle.

Many Ancient Greek vases are orange decorated with black figures.

Pegasus

Pegasus was the legendary flying horse in Greek myths. Use quite a soft pencil to draw him (find out about types of pencil on page 30). The tips below should help.

Do the outline first. Don't try to do it in one go. Draw a bit then look at the picture again.

Compare parts. Are his legs as long as his wings? How long is his neck compared to his body, and so on?

Shade with light pencil strokes.

Draw curved lines for feathers.

Do lots of strokes for the mane.

Go over darker shadows twice.

Back and tail are shaded by the wings.

Shade the muscle in his neck.

Under parts are in shadow.

Unicorn ✏ Horn

You could draw a unicorn. It is like a horse with a single horn.

You can only partly see legs on the far side.

*Or you could use black wax crayon, as on page 57.

Animal monsters

People have always made monsters out of animals, like the Minotaur on the previous page. Here are some more, and a game to help you make your own.

Tail

Make ripples by colouring with corrugated cardboard under your paper.

Do as many humps as you like. Make them smaller as they go away from you.

Loch Ness monster

Legend says that a monster lives in Loch Ness in Scotland. This is what it is traditionally supposed to look like.

Chimaera

The mythical Greek Chimaera had a lion's head, a goat's body and a serpent's tail. Try using different drawing materials for the different parts, as explained below.

Use pencil crayons for the head. Mix strokes of brown, orange, yellow and black for the mane to make it shaggy.

Chalk is good for the hairy goat's body. Smudge brown chalk all over, then use charcoal for details and shading.

Smudge shadow under legs.

Legs shaggy at the top.

Use felt tips on the serpent's tail for contrast. Use two shades of green and put black scales on top.

Do hooves and outline black.

Shapes to draw

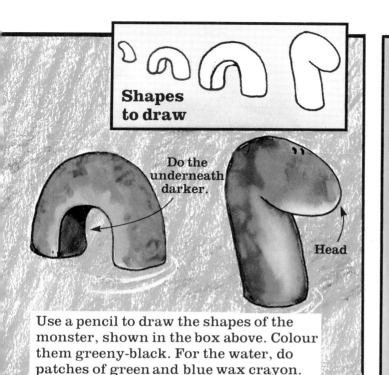

Do the underneath darker.

Head

Use a pencil to draw the shapes of the monster, shown in the box above. Colour them greeny-black. For the water, do patches of green and blue wax crayon. Lay the crayons on their sides and rub.

Animal monsters game

Make your own strange animal monsters by playing this game.

Draw a head at the top of a sheet of paper. It can be a real animal's head, or an imaginary one. Fold the paper so only the end of the neck can be seen.

Pass it to a friend, who adds a body. Fold again so just the end of the body is seen.

Pass the paper on. Someone else adds legs. Unfold the paper to see your creation.

King Kong

King Kong is quite modern, but is already legendary. Try drawing this picture starring him.

Draw the skyscrapers. It is as if you are above them so you can see their roofs. They get narrower as they stretch away from you towards the street below.

Draw the giant gorilla emerging from behind the buildings.* He is dark, but paler underneath where he is lit from the street. Make it night to add atmosphere.

Clouds and moon.

Small plane for King Kong to grab.

*See pages 58-59 for some ways to make him look big.

People or monsters?

All the monsters on these two pages are people of a kind - or at least, they might be.

Yeti

Yetis live in the Himalayas. Nobody knows if they are a type of person, ape or monster. Draw this one on blue paper.or paint a blue background.

Paint a shaggy Yeti with white paint on a brush. Use as little water as possible so the paint is quite dry and goes on in rough streaks. Add a blizzard whirling round him.

He seems to blend into the snow.

Werewolf

This ordinary man turns into a werewolf on nights with a full moon. Colour him with pencil crayons. Use light layers of brown, yellow and pink for skin, and shades of brown for hair.

As he changes, it is as if his face is pulled forward: make his nose longer and his chin stick out; give him a thinner, longer mouth; do his ear pointed and higher up; make him sprout hair on chin, cheeks and forehead.

Fully changed, he is like a fierce wolf. Draw a wolf's muzzle. Add sharp teeth and glowing red eyes. His ears are now on top of his head. He is hairy all over.

You can make a blizzard by spraying white paint from a toothbrush, as on page 57.

66

Frankenstein's monster

Frankenstein stitched together a sort of man and brought him to life artificially. He escaped and terrorized the neighbourhood. This is a portrait of him.

This picture is lit from above. The shadows are black blocks. Copy the shapes in pencil then colour them black. Practise drawing faces like this from newspaper pictures. They often look like blocks of light and shadow.

Lit from above, there are deep shadows in the eye sockets and under the nose, lower lip and chin.

Eerie light experiment

To see the dramatic shadows that light can cast on your face, try this:

Sit in a dark room in front of a mirror and shine a torch from different angles on to your face.

Compare the shadows you see in the mirror with those in the pictures below. They are most dramatic when the light shines from over your head or below your chin. Also note how the shadow of your body is cast on the wall behind you.*

Portrait of a vampire

Vampires rise from the dead and drink human blood. Draw the famous vampire, Count Dracula, like this:

Draw his head and cloak and colour them with crayons. He has red eyes, fangs and a ghastly green skin. Do eerie black face shadows as shown.

Do a shadow behind Dracula, the same shape, only bigger. Use paint or felt tip so it is blacker than he is.

Try copying the two small Dracula figures on the right and add shadows to match.

Lit from below, the shadows are on the upper lip, cheekbones and forehead.

*See more special effects on pages 28-29.

Mechanical monsters

On these two pages are ways to draw robots and other machine-like monsters.

Destructobot

This destructobot is quite hard to draw. Try using a grid to help, like this:

Draw a grid of squares in pencil, as at the bottom of this page. Do the squares as big as you like.

Look at the squares one at a time. Copy the shapes in each one on to the same square in your grid. Then rub out the grid lines.

The labels round the picture show you some details.

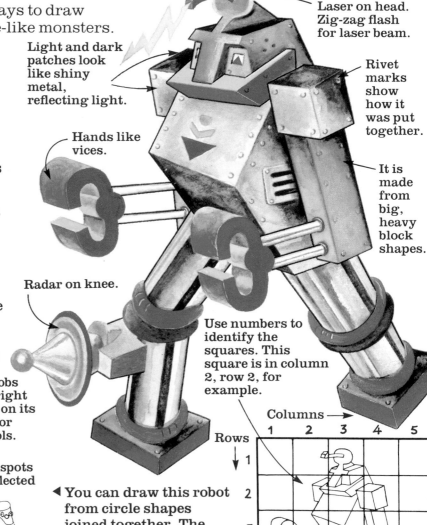

Laser on head. Zig-zag flash for laser beam.

Light and dark patches look like shiny metal, reflecting light.

Rivet marks show how it was put together.

Hands like vices.

It is made from big, heavy block shapes.

Radar on knee.

Use numbers to identify the squares. This square is in column 2, row 2, for example.

Columns →

Rows ↓

Rogue robot

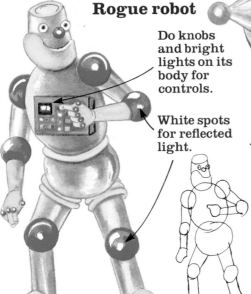

Do knobs and bright lights on its body for controls.

White spots for reflected light.

◀ You can draw this robot from circle shapes joined together. The small picture shows you the shapes to use. Draw them in pencil first.

Before you colour it, rub out the parts of the lines that are not there in the big picture.

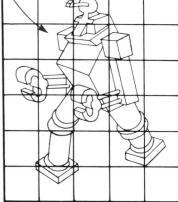

Put a grid on tracing paper over other monsters in this book to help copy them.

Machine mixer

This monster is made from parts of machines. Try to draw a similar one and shade it with dots and lines.

Use dots on rounded parts. The closer the dots, the darker the shadows.

Use lines on flat bits. Criss-cross lines make darker shadows.

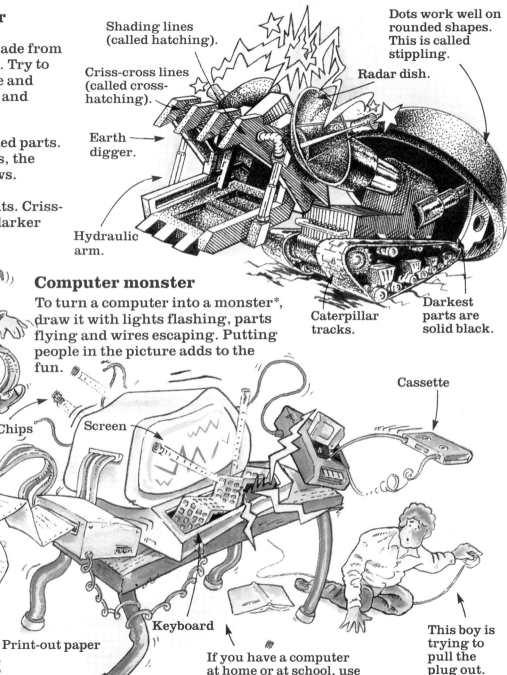

Shading lines (called hatching).

Criss-cross lines (called cross-hatching).

Dots work well on rounded shapes. This is called stippling.

Radar dish.

Earth digger.

Hydraulic arm.

Caterpillar tracks.

Darkest parts are solid black.

Computer monster

To turn a computer into a monster*, draw it with lights flashing, parts flying and wires escaping. Putting people in the picture adds to the fun.

Cassette

Chips

Screen

This flex has swept a boy off his feet.

Print-out paper

Keyboard

If you have a computer at home or at school, use it as a model.

This boy is trying to pull the plug out.

*See more ways to make machines look like monsters on pages 54-55.

69

Techniques and materials

Here is a round up of all the techniques and materials in this part. The chart on the right has a column for each material telling you how you can use it. A white panel across more than one column refers to all the materials in those columns.

Red

Red and yellow make orange.

Yellow
Blue

Mix red, yellow and blue to make brown.

Blue and red make purple.

Yellow and blue make green.

Mixing colours

This colour monster shows you which colours mix to make other colours. You only need red, yellow and blue to make all these colours. (Felt tips do not mix like this). Use black to make them darker and white to make them paler.

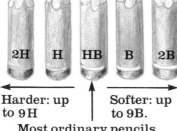

2H   H   HB   B   2B

Harder: up to 9H.   Softer: up to 9B.

Most ordinary pencils to write with are HB.

The pencil family

Pencils can be hard or soft. Soft pencils make thick, fuzzy lines. Hard pencils make thin, clear lines. Most pencils are marked with a code to tell you how hard or soft they are. See how the code works on the right.

Using fixative sprays

Fixative sprays stop pictures in soft materials like charcoal, chalk and soft pencil smudging. They come in aerosol cans and you can get them from art suppliers. Never breathe the spray or work near a flame. It is best to use them outside, since they smell very strong. Do not throw empty cans on a fire.

Pencil crayons	Pencils	
Pencil crayons are good for doing hairy effects (see pages 64 and 66).	You probably use pencils the most. You can draw with them first even if you colour afterwards.	

Drawing lines

Use the point of crayons, pencils or charcoal pencils for fine lines and the side of the point for fuzzy lines and shading.

Shading with lines and dots

You can shade areas with lines and dots. See an example of this on page 69.

 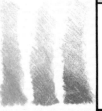

 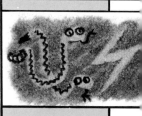

Make different shades with pencil crayon by pressing lighter or harder.

Textures

Make textures by rubbing over things placed under your paper (see pages 47 and 64).

Charcoal	Chalk	Wax crayons	Paint	Ink	Felt tips

Shading

Lie a stick of charcoal, chalk or a wax crayon on its side and rub. Snap the sticks to make them smaller if you need to.

Spots and splashes

Paint and ink are liquid (paint may be powdery or hard but you add water to use it). Drop blobs of paint from a brush (see page 53), or shake ink blots from a nib. Spray paint or ink from an old toothbrush (see pages 51 and 66).

Using the side of the point.

Chalk shows up well on black paper.

Use chalk to help make double prints (page 50).

Scrape shapes into layers of wax crayon (page 57) or into paint on top of wax (page 63).

Thick felt tips are good for making solid areas of colour. Thin ones are good for lines and details.

Hatching

Draw lines like this across the part you want to shade.

Cross-hatching

Draw two sets of lines criss-crossing for darker shadows.

Stippling

Shade with dots. More dots, closer together, make darker areas.

Smudging

Smudge soft pencils, chalk and charcoal with your finger. (See the fuzzy monster on page 51, for example.) Use it for fire, clouds, fur and so on.

Use wax crayons and chalk to make double prints, as on page 50.

Washes

Make a wash background with streaks of paint or ink on paper soaked with water. See how on page 53.

Using a rubber

Use a rubber to make marks in pencils, charcoal and chalk. See an example on page 49.

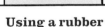

Wax and water don't mix. You can use this to make good contrasts (see page 53).

Prints

Dip your fingers in paint or ink and make prints. See some ways to use them on pages 44 and 56. Try making prints with other things, such as those shown below.

Felt tips come in lots of colours — even luminous ones — but they do not mix well. You can use dark ones on top of light ones, though.

Try using coins, feathers, wood. Textures show best with crayons, pencils, charcoal or chalk.

Cotton reel
Matchbox
Polystyrene chip

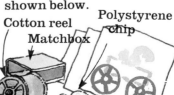

Index

animal, 32, 33
   monsters, 43, 44, 64-65
animation, 2, 34-37
anthropomorphism, 54
arms, 4, 5, 39

baby, 18
bird's eye view, 11
borders, 25

car, convertible, 55
caricatures, 2, 8-9, 16
cartoon
   films, 2, 34-37
   jokes, 22-23
   story books, 2, 30-31
cel, 36, 37
Cerberus, 43
children, 18
Chimaera, 64
comic strips, 26-27
cooker, crazy, 54

destructobot, 68
dinosaur, 25, 46-47
Dracula, 67
dragons, 56-57
dwarfs, 60

ears, 3, 6
explosions, 28
expressions, 6-7, 38
eyes, 3, 6, 8

feet, 4
fingerprints, 44, 56
fish, 33, 53
fixative spray, 70
flying monsters, 47
foreshortening, 11
Frankenstein's monster, 67

ghosts, 48-49
giants, 58-59
goblins, 61
graveyard phantom, 49

hair, 3, 8, 9, 38
hands, 4, 39
Hergé, 30-31
household horrors, 54
human horrors, 60-61

in-betweeners, 36

key pictures, 35, 36, 37
King Kong, 65
kitchen shapes, 54

legs, 4, 5, 39
lettering, 24
light box, 36
lighting effects, 28
Loch Ness monster, 64

Martian, 50
materials, 23, 42, 70-71
mechanical monsters, 68-69
Medusa, 62
mermaid, 62
Minotaur, 63
mixed monsters, 45
monster shapes, 44-45
mouth, 3, 8
movement, 12-14
   lines, 12, 13, 14
mythical monsters, 62-63, 64

noses, 3, 6, 8, 9

octopus, giant, 52
ogre, 59
old people, 19

pencils, 23, 70
people, drawing, 40, 58
perspective, 14, 20-21, 59, 61
profile, 3
   three-quarter, 7
projector, 34

robots, 68
rostrum camera, 37

scenery, 20-21, 26, 27, 31, 37
script, 26, 27
sea monsters, 52-53
shape figures, 5, 12, 16
shooting, 36
shutter, 34
silhouettes, 14, 28, 29
single cartoons, 22-23
skeleton, 60
sound effects, 25, 26, 28, 35
space aliens, 50-51
special effects, 28-29
speech bubbles, 24, 25, 27, 29
stereotypes, 16-17
stick figures, 4-5, 12, 13, 16
storyboard, 35
strip cartoon, 2, 24-25, 29

techniques, 70-71
Tintin, 2, 30-31

unicorn, 63

vanishing point, 20
vampire, 22, 67

Walt Disney, 34
werewolf, 66
worm's eye view, 11

Yeti, 66

First published in 1987 by Usborne Publishing Ltd,
Usborne House, 83–85 Saffron Hill, London EC1N 8RT, England.

Copyright © Usborne Publishing Ltd. 1987

The name Usborne and the device 🏺 are Trade Marks of
Usborne Publishing Ltd.

Printed in Great Britain.